Crossroads to Destiny

© 2020 by Sandra Gallimore

ISBN **978-1-947514-29-4**

Printed in the United States of America

St. Clair Publications
P. O. Box 726
McMinnville, TN 37111-0726

http://stclairpublications.com

Cover Design

Spencer St. Clair

CROSSROADS TO

DESTINY

A NOVELLA OF LIFE

Sandra Gallimore

Edited by Stanley J. St. Clair

Crossroads to Destiny

Chapter One

August 2018

St. Louis, Missouri

Nothing diminishes 'clean and fresh,' like sweating bullets in the sun when one is trying to make a good impression. But now I am about to unload my clean and fresh handmade products for the flea market, a popular activity in the city. I have an eerie feeling that there is something mystical about this day. I determine that today I must really take Helen Keller's words to heart: "Optimism is the faith that leads to achievement." That's a very elevated and elegant way of saying you better believe in yourself if you hope to accomplish anything you want to. You gotta love great quotes, and there is nothing like a dose of Helen Keller to inspire you on a hot August day in St. Louis.

This is not a day to enjoy all the interesting items here, to enjoy the market myself, but to make a little voodoo happen in this August sun in order to pay my mall store rent. Discontinued stock I have not sold this year must go at half-price today to take the heat off my bank balance. These days more people are saving money at flea markets than going to malls. I am under contract to one but pay twenty dollars to the other. Here, I get a table and chair, and several hundred people for a captive audience, the results will be two-fold for my struggling natural soaps and perfumes business. Instant income for older stock that would take up space in my store, as well as product advertisement and recognition to several hundred people at one time. It is hard work for any vendor but the benefits can be many.

I pull into the parking lot and see about half the vendors are already setting up. Pity the several I see unloading heavy goods in the already oppressive sun at eight-thirty in the morning.

The summer of 2018 has heralded an obvious heat wave that offers a definite different conclusion than Washington's drumbeat, 'No proof of accelerated climate change,' echoing on social media, and in politics. Really? Well I say no matter what the talking heads say, Midwest August is notably dog days, and this month is seeing many thirsty pups. It is sure not a time to be selling handmade soap and perfume at one of our great flea markets I know but Helen Keller wouldn't let a little sunburn stop her and neither will I.

As I start unloading my boxes on the six-foot table I am doing just what Helen encourages her readers to do. I'm keeping the faith in my products and my skill, and working to get my business out of the red, back on track. Luckily, today I brought an ice-filled thermal chest to keep my products from melting in this ninety-degree plus day. My store assistant could be doing this thankless job but this is older stock, I know how to price it in order to move it from my hand to the customer's. That is what will make next month's last lease payment on the mall store.

Flea markets are a great place for me to impress grocery store soap addicts with my lovely lavender or honeysuckle bars. Not French milled, but close; and some have the benefits of goat's milk, which solves almost everyone's dry skin or allergy issues. No secret ingredients for shelf life in natural soaps for me, I like natural in unique perfumes and potions. And that is my store name as plain and natural as it can be. 'Perfumes and Potions.' Kinda witchy, huh? It brings the curious in and then they are smitten with the products. Or at least that is the idea. The mall brings in the people on a day to day basis, but it is hard to compete with the competitor prices of a chain store. They can offer products at reduced prices because of the thousands that sit in warehouses for months waiting to be marketed a year later as 'this month's special.'

The freshly made soaps and lotions, and yes, potions, cost a little more and feel a little fresher without the extra ingredients to preserve. But back to the flea market with droves of folks coming in already, braving the sun to see all the antiques, clothes, jewelry, comic books and whatever else. I'm pushing perfume in the sun, selling soap in the shade. It's not a day to challenge Ol' Sol in St. Louis.

The mall contract ending means I need to decide to open my business somewhere else, add another location, or even go out of business... maybe go back to Bloomington. Indiana is my home. I just need to decide if there is anything to go back for since my parents are gone. Might take some classes at IU again. Bloomington, Indiana is a great little University town with plenty of country outside the city limits and culture inside it, a college town with a population of everything from farmers to professors. Sometimes they can be both. An ideal place for culture in a peaceful atmosphere. But St. Louis has many of the same attractions, Midwest friendly. I am at somewhat of a standstill if the truth is known. Restless, do not quite know where I want to go from here, at the 'been there-done that' stage, I guess.

Meanwhile, in the here and now, selling this old stock will take that worry off me; I should have a final month of store sales that will then be the year's profit.

Then comes the decision — what to do? The poem of the 'road best taken' comes to mind so I must choose it, whatever it may be. I can't stand still and stagnate; maybe I'll stay another year if the mall loses a cheaper competitor here at contract end. Other businesses may have to walk away too.

Malls are losing customers due to the economy. Traffic has been dwindling — that is a fact. But on this day, I can only think of going where it is not hot. Where is it not hot? I'll find somewhere that at least has three out of the four seasons going for it. We vendors are doing well already this morning; even see some old customers who stop to replenish their favorites of my soaps at sale prices. They are happy now, and I'm beginning to feel better too. That optimism for you. Thanks again, Helen, I needed to be reminded. I daub a fingerprint of lavender oil on each temple now that I am set up, smiling, and selling. I planned, brought plenty of change and dollar bills. The lavender oil makes me feel cool, refreshed if only for a moment. This air is almost steaming with this many people milling around. I see them walk by looking wet, tired, and uncomfortable. They seem to be dedicated to finding their next bargain.

The aroma of all these bodies is in the air and beginning to float around the ether now. I push forward a couple of spray bottles of sage, elder, and rose water on the table, meant to cool the brave souls who stop at my table. I subtly spray some in the air especially around my area. They are picking up the bottles that say 'free' as I encourage each one to spray liberally, knowing they will feel much better in the heat. An ancient herbal combination—as the saying goes, 'you should bottle it.' Well I have, and here it is.

I push my long hair back and look in my purse for a random hair tie, slip it on my wrist until I have time to pull my hair off my neck. The sun is relentless. I should have rigged a beach umbrella. I take some melting honeysuckle soap off the table; pack it back on the ice while no one sees. I decide to place some perfume samples and better selling amulets of perfume on the table with new matching soap and lotions. The colors are inviting, and I can tell by people's faces that the fragrances are wafting out to the crowd as they pass me. It is a good feeling to see them stop in their tracks to see what it is. The aromas compete with the food venders and their spells of good things—elephant ears, roasted corn, chicken on a stick, huge breaded pork fritters. I should not complain of the heat when I see the cooks standing over hot oil pots in this weather. Their red faces are testimony to their hard work.

Folks are stopping to try my samples, spraying the herbs and going through the basket of books and potions I have in the middle of the table. I stand up again to attend to their purchases, so glad the clothes I wore are the right ones in the heat. It's not a normal thing for me to wear hippie type clothes but this loose top and gathered long skirt are just the things for air flow. My gypsy appearance probably helps the potion illusion too. I feel rather exotic, cute, little bit mysterious if a little sweaty underneath the mystique.

I wrap some Patchouli bath oils, plus lotion, for a customer, take out a package of aloe throw-away wipes for those who spot them, and use one myself to wipe my hands. It cools the pulse points on the wrists. A few drops of lavender oil on my temples, or rosewater, in between customers is the saving grace as I see other sellers wiping brows and fanning themselves with paper fans that read 'Farm Bureau Coop.'

When I sit down again…that is when I see him. He is leaning against a wooden stage where they make announcements to the crowd. He is staring at me intently, seems like for some time, watching my clean-up ritual. He smiles at being caught watching. I nod back; take the hair tie off my wrist, self-conscience of my melting hairdo.

He has dark curly hair just over his sea foam blue seersucker shirt collar. I like that. He has dressed wisely for the weather too. He has a handsome face, rugged, open and inviting. I wish he would look away, but then customers gather to occupy me, block my view. I get a quick glimpse of him looking cool as a cucumber, under that big elm tree next to the stage. He seems amused, still smiling as he watches me explain my products to several ladies who have come together to see what I have. They are a few friends comparing notes on what they have used and like. This is what I like, to show people the mixtures of flowers and oils that provide help besides fragrance for the body. This is what I know, what I have learned in France, and in my own research. The ancient art of herbs and flowers for health, for food, life, and for enjoyment. By then I had almost forgotten the tall, handsome drink of water under the tree, while I am busy enjoying these ladies, their stories of potions their grandmothers made.

The sizable sales are welcome too. I wrap up the rest of the Opium soap made from poppies, brought today for a lady who was happy to get her favorite at a very reduced price. It's my favorite soap too, you sell more of what you like and display. She leaves with lotion to match, then both of us are pleased. I look up but the handsome lad is gone. 'Just my luck,' I think, as I put the money box away under my chair.

Not a man has ventured over to my table yet. Of course, the men I see on a constant basis are buying perfumes for wives and girlfriends, not conducive to an exciting social life in my business. A shadow suddenly blocks the sun and there he stands, shielding it from my face. He holds two big cups. "Your choice, Madam, ice water or iced tea, or both."

I am stunned, but grateful. "Iced tea sounds wonderful," I babble, "Are you some knight in shining armor?" I laugh.

He smiles and makes an exaggerated bow to me, "Well, it's sure not a day for armor, but if you need to be rescued, I'm here."

Little did he know just how much I needed to be rescued, for many reasons. We chat between customers, fun talking but hard to concentrate on soap and sales. His name is Chris, he says, short for Christopher. His mother named him after Superman, Christopher Reeve. He looks better than superman, a real dream date, actually. He asks if I am a witch, a voodoo woman with all these potions. I tell him if am, I am still waiting for the magic to happen.

His comeback both startles and amuses me. "It's here," he says, without a smile, "I'm here."

"Does that really work for you... ever?"

His turn to laugh, "It could just be true, you know."

There is a comfortable silence, I put more books in

the basket of sale items I have in the middle of the table.

"What was that stuff you put on your temples?" he finally asks.

"It's just a touch of Lavender oil," I say, "It refreshes and is helpful for headaches from stress."

He starts rummaging through the books in the basket. "I'm pretty drawn to you," he says, in a matter-of-fact way as he looks at each book.

I chuckle, try to keep it light. "Maybe it's just a little sunstroke," I say, as I straighten the table.

"Seriously, I'd like to spend some time with you, get to know you, out of the sun," he says. "You're not attached to anyone are you, I hope?"

I shake my head and the clip I have managed to jam in to hold it falls back out.

"Here, allow me." He gently gathers up the loose hair, gives it a quick twist and clips the thing snugly to the top of my head. He absent-mindedly fluffs my hair, catches a lose curl, tucks it in, then steps back and takes a drink of ice water. I let my breath out slowly, quietly. It was the most intimate touch I had ever had from a man. Sexier than any sex act could ever be. Erotic without meaning to be.

He squats down and pulls the basket over to the

edge. "How much are the books? This one about ginseng looks interesting. *Ginseng and the Plants that Make You Money*," he reads out loud.

I tell him they are all five dollars.

He reaches in his pocket and brings out a five-dollar bill. "Any tax?"

I shake my head. "Not in this state."

"I'll take it." He stands up, hands me the money and shoves the book under one muscular arm. "You will see me again, won't you? Today? After the market closes?"

"Uh, well I might, but I don't know anything about you, do I?"

He shifts to the other leg, shrugs his broad shoulders. "Well, I know all I need to know about you, just to have dinner. I think maybe you know too. I think we both know magic if, and when, we see it... you're blushing, you know."

I laugh it off. "Nah, you should realize by now I got a little sunburn today!"

He smiles that Tom Cruise smile. "I'll be here at five, is that when it ends?"

I nod and smile back as he walks away. He turns and calls back to me... a good distance away now. "Oh, I don't even know your name?"

"It's in the book!" I call back to him and he smiles that killer smile. Now let me sit down to rest my shaky legs.

It's my habit to write in the first page of the books, a saying I had heard many years back just to inspire customers to come back. It tends to work so they tell me. He is gone and I already regret it. 'What a character,' I think while watching until he disappears in the crowded parking lot. 'Wonder if he really will come back?' He was right, I do know all I need to know. It felt like magic.

Chapter Two

St. Louis, Missouri

August 2018

Chris

I grab a burger on the way home thinking about the pretty lady at the market, wrack my brain for a suitable place to have dinner. It needs to be quiet so I can talk to her. One with good food but not ostentatious. What a doll! Smart, quick with comebacks but delicate looking. She's a risk taker, that I can tell, but not too showy. I like that. I guess I just like her. There is something different about her. It felt right, felt a little magical, maybe just because I wasn't expecting it. Just the combo of those fragrances and that white peasant blouse. She'll want to change though, maybe she'll just want to go to a casual place.

I'll wear a white shirt and dress jeans until we talk about it. I can grab a quick shower, sure need one in this heat, pick up some flowers too. But what kind for this sort of mysterious young lady who works with flowers all day? Maybe daffodils. Mom loves those and they are not too pushy, like roses, they seem like gentle flowers. She seemed gentle herself, very pretty lady with sparkly green eyes, that's all I know. Damn! Why didn't I ask what her favorite flowers are?

I throw my stuff on the couch and check the phone, going through the messages. Business, business, Mom, Mom. Mom… again. I hear her crying on the line. Dad is in the hospital! I call back and she's not home. Doesn't she have a phone with her? Must be the hospital phone number she's calling from, it's not theirs. I leave a message that I am taking the first plane out. What could it be? His heart? He just had a check-up. Said it was okay.

I grab a quick shower and throw a few things in a carry-on, call the airport and book the next flight to San Francisco, just have time to go back and tell the lady why I have to cancel, but I don't even know her name. So, she said it was in the book. I throw it in the bag too.

I call a cab to go to the market venue. Four-thirty. We sit in traffic what seems like a long time. I tell the driver to take a short cut, I am really worried about Dad, he is at that age…. old. We finally get there, five-fifteen. I tell the driver to stay there for the airport run and promise a good tip. People are packing up and leaving. I hurry to where I remember her spot is, it is bare. She's gone.

Damn! I ask the people packing up in the next spot. They say she left early... said she had a headache. I need to get back to the cab. I will have to find her store later, apologize... but she did leave early. Surely dad will be fine, he is in the right place to be fine.

The cab heads to the airport and I dig out her book, my book, out of the bag just to occupy my mind. I look for her name, but I don't see it anywhere. I flip to the front, see someone has written something, maybe a dedication for a gift to someone. I read the very neat writing, it is in green ink... 'When the time is right you will see a path, if you follow it, there you will find your destiny.' Well, that's one to really think about. I am sort of on a new path, I guess, just got waylaid as I took the first step... 1 will come back and find her. I would bet she is on the path I am looking for. I should be thinking about Dad instead; he needs me. We have always been so close, nothing left unsaid between us, but still, he'll be worried about Mom if he's very sick. Well, I'm on my way, that's one good thing.

On the plane the passengers are subdued, quietly resting and relaxing as they commute from a day at work, a tiring vacation, or — like me, on an unplanned family emergency. I hope it turns out right for all of us. I have a mixed drink on my tray as we wait for dinner to be served. I enjoy the little perks, privileges of first class after a few years of crowded egg carton traveling on the cheap. I've earned it, and I've learned in this time to pace myself and not to fall prey to the pitfalls of success, mainly that success itself can be the biggest pitfall if you don't put it in perspective. You can always want more, or you can stop and enjoy what you've already made happen. You can enjoy the simplicity of one or two drinks to relax, to value socializing with it — to discuss business informally, or you can let it, or any number of other negatives, be your reward and distract you from what you wanted in the first place. Most of this I learned from Dad, from working with him.

Dad's work ethic is what he has given to me if I had to name one thing only. It's a fine line a man must draw in life in order to be that kind of successful. The kind where it is enough; where you don't have to compete with anything but a goal of your own, or even just the vision of a goal that you can be satisfied you have reached. Dad has given me this in so many ways. He's been my mentor, an example. I think he knows this because he set out to do it. He let me decide what I wanted to do and, without my knowing it he mentored me as I was doing it.

It took me a few years to figure that out. I smile to myself, lean back, close my eyes and try to bring up a mental picture of the lady with no name. It's the eyes I see, and then fade-in to the face. The sparkling clear green eyes. I read somewhere that only one percent of the world's people have green eyes. How does that happen? So, she is in the one percent. I'll buy that. As we say, she seems like a keeper. Personality, smarts, and looks. That is the triple threat. What the hell am I doing? Dad's in the hospital and I'm thinking about a woman, maybe not just any woman though. I wonder if it's his heart, he's too heavy for one thing. Mom will have to keep him on a diet.

We land in the brilliant lights of San Francisco, always home to come back to after my business travels. I grab my carry-on and race to the waiting cabs and hold up a twenty-dollar bill. "Who wants a tip for getting me to hospital through all the short cuts?" I say out loud.

A driver jumps in his cab and says, "Let's go," and we do.

"Hurry, man," I tell him, "I don't know how much time I have." He nods and steps on the gas.

He earns his tip as we get there in what must be record time. I pay him and lunge for the automatic emergency door, but it is too late. My God, it must be too late! Mom is there in the outer waiting room, not with Dad. It's the look on her face that tells the story. Her face is blank as she tells me he died about an hour ago, and here she still sits. I can see she's in shock.

I guide her to a more private cardiac waiting area. I slump down beside her not wanting to hear the details, but she tells them because she must. It's all grim reality. A need to relate every detail, to hold on to it. It is all one can control under the circumstances. I let her go on because she needs to go on. I wasn't there when he needed me, that's all I can think in my own shock, didn't think he would die but he has. There was nothing left to say, but he was alone. Seems like no one should be alone. He had Mom. Was it enough? I hope it was enough.

I need a long quiet time to think of what I don't want to think about. Does that make sense? No, it's the broken logic of grief and I feel it too keenly. Her face is a blank. There have been no tears yet because she is stunned. But mine come.

"I didn't know what to do," she says quietly. "I just waited for you to come and tell me what to do."

I put my arm around her. "We'll go home," I tell her. "That's all we need to do right now. I'll help you... I'll help you with everything." I put my arms around her as she cries out her heartbreak.

"I'm glad I waited for you; I didn't know what to do."

"Mom, I'm here now," I say gently. I realize it's the

second time that day I say "I'm here" to a woman.

We go home to the house they have lived in for fifty years. I fix her a hot toddy even though it's August. I put a goodly amount of brandy in it to relax her. She drinks it, nods that she will lie down for a while. I collapse in a home that feels strange to me. I have not lived here for many years. It feels like a tomb now. I fix myself a strong seven and seven, decide to sit in Dad's chair with its same old collapsed cushion, the soiled arm covers to protect the original material. How many times did we try to get him a new chair? But now I want to feel him there, in this one, his good old chair. It still feels warm from him. He has sat in it just a few hours ago. The last human contact even if is just heat. He is imprinted all these years later, but the silence in the room is deafening.

I reach for my bag. I want to read that message in the book again. Maybe it will help Mom, and me, at a time like this. I reach in... but... no book there. It is gone. I realize I have left it in the taxi. It slid from the side pocket of my bag. I'll call the cab company, but I don't even know the name of the cab, too much in a hurry to jump out. I've lost the ginseng book, the woman, and my dad all in one day. The entire day feels like I am in daze, like it was all a dream, and now more of a nightmare.

Mom is back up, can't sleep. She wants to fix me dinner. I am as far from hunger as one can be, but I say yes just so she will be busy and get tired enough to sleep tonight. We will both try to ease the pain for each other; that's part of the camaraderie for the survivors. But I must realize this is more of a finality for her. I have my whole life to live, Dad was her whole life. She must feel it is over for her too when she might live several more years. It will take a while, but she must go on, I'll have to encourage her.

I don't know how women do it... I've seen it in the insurance business many a time. Life is over for them twenty, even thirty years after the husband dies, and they sit there more or less, waiting to die too. They don't realize, or many don't, that they are a person, in their own right. They are more than wife, mother, grandmother, aunt. They once had wishes and dreams of their own but now those don't enter their mind as being important. My mom will be the same way, I have no doubt. This is way too much thinking for me right now.

"Come to dinner," Mom says. I'll tell her about the lady and the book. We must talk about something besides Dad.

The next day in between all the other phone calls I call her store, remembering she said the name 'Perfumes and Potions.' It rings busy both times I try and then I am covered up with family details. It is a week until I have a moment to breath from the funeral and estate business. I have called the store number twice more but still get a busy signal. Meantime, I realize I am here for the long haul. If I'm doing right by Mom it means staying here to help for a while, it's not like I need to work, but I won't give up on the lady in St. Louis.

I put Dad's chair in my old room, so Mom won't have the constant reminder he is not in it. And I admit, I've talked to him when I am alone. I tell him I will find you, voodoo lady, wherever the path will lead... I know Dad would want me to, I know I want to follow a path I never knew existed.

Chapter Three

October 10, 2018

Panama City Beach, Florida
Elsie

Landfall at 1:30 P.M., says the National Weather Service. It is the first information we have had this morning. The Gulf Coast is bracing for a hurricane and it's only halfway through our week-long vacation in Panama City Beach.

It is sure to be a direct hit, so says the Weather Channel. They see it coming ashore on the beach, where we are staying. If that isn't scary enough they say the entire area is in the hurricane's path. Hurricane Michael, they call it.

It's a terrifying prospect for the three of us, away from home in a strange place. We watch the alerts instead of going to the beach. My friends Charlene and Mary, a male friend of theirs and I have put our resources together to rent this vacation condo on the beach, my first vacation in three years.

I call home to tell Mom what is happening. I know

she must be watching the weather and worrying about me. Of course, she says to come home, "just get out of there." But we want to see if a few days of vacation can be saved. We're not stupid, though, just waiting on more information.

Unlike my friends with me, I do not have a job back in Trenton I can go back to. A few of us have been replaced with artificial intelligence in the shipping business. Some have saved their severance pay while I thought I deserved a vacation for my loyalty to the company, only to be tossed out like the trash. So much for how my loyalty has paid off, and now the vacation is kaput.

After ten years I am now in Trenton's unemployment line. Forced by technology and time to learn a new skill in my fourth decade and to compete with thousands of other computer pros looking for work, along with new graduate classes with even higher skills than the rest of us.

This vacation was to lie on the beach and decide what avenue might be my future, a rather dismal prospect. Right now, all I can think of is 'getting out of Dodge' as the National Weather Service is updating the storm to a Cat three now. I don't want to find out what happens in a Cat three.

We finally reach John, the other ladies' friend, and say we are heading to a shelter, as directed, because the storm is getting worse. We tell him we hope to have some vacation left after the storm is over if they miss their mark at NWS. John is staying with friends he met at the hotel next door. They are going to 'ride it out,' as they say here on the beach, 30 stories up. "No way," we three say about that. We girls throw our bags in the car and are on the road by nine o'clock this morning.

The two main streets on the beach, Front Beach Road and Hwy 98, are packed, as cars head inland to beat the storm. The race is on now to find gas, food, water, and somewhere to stay. We will all have to keep driving to find any of that, but now we all sit in lines of traffic miles long. It's a race against the impact of the storm set to hit in the next few hours.

And this is where we are until we can find shelter C by following the arrows. Turns out that Shelter C is almost twenty miles away from the beach, across one of the bridges to a gymnasium outside Panama City. Where the heck were shelters A and B? We finally find where to go after getting lost, caught in traffic trying to get across the bridge. We follow the arrows on the road and turn into a complex of school buildings, one looking the biggest, with many cars parked there already. Now we need to find the right door to get in as the wind is already gusting hard enough to bend the sapling trees around this school in half. All the doors seem to be locked down, so there we stand like Dorothy, kicking the door, trying to get in the storm shelter with Auntie Em. No, that was a tornado. Finally, we find a door with men coming out. They seem to be tying things down outside; helping other people get inside. This is shelter C. It is eleven o'clock and it is already crowded, two hours until landfall.

We see it is a gymnasium with a crowd of people spreading blankets on the wooden gym floor. Here is the Red Cross with their table set up with bottles of water, papers for each person filing by to fill out in order to account for every single person coming into a shelter from the hurricane. It's kind of reassuring to see them.

Now we're in the line too, taking our water and paperwork like everyone else. Shelter seekers keep coming in a steady bedraggled stream behind us, whole families wet and dragging whatever they can carry, blankets, food in bags, stuffed bears. The gym floor, hard as a rock, is covered with humanity already, a noisy din of activity as people find a space on the floor and get settled. We find a little open hole of space between people to sit down in a circle, put our three purses in the middle of us in this sea of strangers from who knows where. We have a couple of blankets that Mary had in her trunk, but we left our bags in the car. Some people have already managed to find, or be given, the few cots they have. A few people look very ill. Others have made makeshift beds on the bleachers on one side of the gym. Many are just sitting on the bleachers with a blanket wrapped around them in the middle of rolling suitcases, and other possessions that must bring some consolation.

Soon the doors will be locked and all of us will be hostage to whatever damage the hurricane decides to inflict. It's another perilous time on the Gulf Coast. The line keeps forming to add to what would be, maybe, a few hundred strangers occupying that limited space.

After the initial shock of settling in passes I look around at the people there. Many seem to be from the city on the Gulf itself. Panama City. They have the clothes of urban poor and middle income residents, garbage bags of what they threw together for their families. There are the upscale here too, travelers with jewelry flashing, mixed in with everyone else's four-foot square space of polished gym floor. No one says they have four feet, it's just the minimum needed for bodies and a few possessions. You can see the culture shock in their faces but that soon disappears. No special treatment exists in a hurricane. Humans are equal beings in a catastrophe, all just trying to survive. Decade after decade, over a hundred years for the Red Cross to stand ready, there to ensure some form of normalcy, protection for those in harm's way. Red is the only color that matters to that organization, the color of bloodshed. There is no supremacy, there is only humanity.

I must admit we three are much like these privileged interlopers, polished vacationers that stick out like a sore thumb in the mass of people. We, too, look like diamonds in a handful of rhinestones but it does not take us long until we no longer feel like fish out of water.

There is no class or color distinction in this gymnasium, just a mish-mash of strangers standing in line for a sandwich and water, a few offering to help others who sit helpless in wheelchairs. All are worried about their homes and property, loved ones, and their own safety. No one knows what will happen or how bad it will be, even in this, hopefully, secure shelter.

We three ladies are no different than the people huddled next to us now, nervous, displaced, amid this sea of strangers. Like others, we talk low; compare our possible losses to these townspeople who face many of these storms every year. They must gamble with destiny every time. Again, they are dodging a bullet, racing to a shelter, but will their homes, schools, and hospitals survive, I wonder? We hear many of their stories around the huge gymnasium, as they tell a few friendly faces about their past experiences, and we talk about our lives back in Trenton. They are curious about us too, and the noise around us is animated with nervous talk, as everyone tries to make some type of nest with what they have.

There's nothing to do but watch the activity of the crowd. Some try to lie down and sleep but there is only room for the fetal position, or maybe that is how they feel like lying right now. We hear the constant questions to the Red Cross volunteers. Everyone hopes they are not in the wrong place at the wrong time in what could be a huge storm. We have no idea because there are no radios or information to be had. This is the time of waiting before the landfall. We hope we have made the right decision twenty miles away from the predicted landfall instead of trying to outrun the storm as many are doing.

The Red Cross nurses and volunteers start a line-up of people to get a sack lunch of sandwich, chips, and little dessert packets of a cookie. This must be to get organized before landfall when the lights go out. People need to be fed, but it is also providing a measure of normalcy. They field more questions giving mostly 'I don't know' for answers, because they don't know, but they will check.

Naturally, all is in limbo until the storm comes ashore and damage can be assessed. As the time gets closer the wind becomes strong enough that we can hear it, even in the gym. The business of eating is a method of keeping people occupied, calm. But many have their own food snacks which they begin to share with others.

Some of us finally get thin mats to lie on in our small

space, with a hopeful promise of cots the next day or two if need be. Wouldn't the storm be over by then, we wonder? What do they mean 'next day or two?' The lights flash a few times then shut down into total darkness. A general shrill cry bursts from the crowd as people freeze where they are. The tension is thick as the heat of humid Florida, because there is no air conditioning in a room with hundreds of people. The generator growls out its noise and the lights pop back on. Somehow, lights had represented safety to all; you can hear the relief in the noisy voices.

But the wind grows stronger. We can hear the gusts through the banging panels and the windows on the roof of the gym. Then windows break and we feel water come in with the wind. This brings another shriek from the crowd. We feel the spray of it through the broken glass. A couple of hours have passed, and we realize this must be it. Landfall.

Water is raining in, but only in the one area now. Someone is climbing up to fix it. The main hurricane must have passed in those few moments, but no one tells us anything even though we see and hear what must be a hundred people inquiring at the Red Cross table. The volunteers are weaving in and out of the people sitting, lying on the floor. They are calm, busy with errands as all activity ceases in the gym. In fact, there is mostly silence for the next few hours. It is amazing how one loses track of time when shut up for a long period. We were not even sure if it was day or night. I realize I have lost track of time while there on the floor.

We try to listen for updates but there is little information even from the uniformed men that came in and out, or the people bringing in supplies for snacks and meals. We seem to be guarded by the men in uniform, which is a rather sobering, yet comforting, feeling. The promised cots do not come after the many hours that pass. Dinner sandwiches are provided, along with more water. People start bedding down for the night with whatever they have piled up to sleep on. A pillow would be a luxury so it is interesting to see how creative folks can be. For all the effort none of it works for us, we just lie there and adapt to the shape of the floor. Flat.

I look around and feel the real meaning of 'misery loves company.' I could swear I hear everyone quietly thinking the same thing... until you have slept on a rock-hard gymnasium floor you cannot know what concrete does to your body. We three use our purses for a semblance of a pillow, sharing the other blanket we had scored with one of the people next to us.

The lights are turned down and silence and air are thick around us until bodies start moving again hours later. Nothing has been heard but an occasional cough, children talking low, and one baby crying most of the night. I can't see where the baby is but it sounds very young, can't imagine how the mother is doing through this ordeal.

Another day seems to have begun with more water and food from the Red Cross table. Still just dribbles of information. It is not what we want to hear. We will not be able to get back to the beach, no one will be allowed because of the damage between here and there. It is obviously terribly bad out there. Our plans will have to change when we are allowed to leave. So far no one is able to venture out in the storm. I see a table with some snacks and fruit that has been brought in. There is a box of magazines and books next to a thermal cooler of milk. A nurse tells me they are bringing items in as they get them, and when the police can get into our area. Everyone must be working hard to find, and provide, for all. Someone else has brought in more boxes of books. One or two people have ventured to sift through them.

From the low conversations I gather it is dangerously bad for miles around, trees and lines down everywhere, cars overturned, etc. No one says it but the faces of the emergency people coming in are grim. The Red Cross is doing a wonderful job in this emergency except that there is simply no information, as people are told over and over. I suspect that this is how they must proceed in this situation, given what they already know, but they know how to keep people calm. If not, this number of people would have dire results if excited.

Time. It is wearing on everyone with nothing to do but think and worry. The children are bored and restless. We're all bored and restless. I walk to the box of books and pick a couple out for myself, Mary, and Charlene. I stop at the table for another bottle of water, take a restroom break. Luckily there are athletes' restrooms right there in the gym, which are already not desirable to use due to the number of people living together over twenty-four hours. We have gone from first class luxury in the condo to a night of trying to catch even an hour of sleep on hard concrete. You would think there would be lots of tossing and turning but most people just lay in defeated lumps, exhausted.

The three of us are desperate to even find a new spot in the gym. The luxury spots to get are along the wall so you can lean back, but they went early and are a premium in a room with bleachers on two sides. Looks like the teenagers had advance knowledge to grab the wall areas. It would have been a way to lean against the wall and sleep. But, as Mary says, at least we are alive, fed, and out of harm's way.

We hear good news from the Red Cross. We are going to get hot food tonight, this second night here, and we are excited. You can feel the energy in the room change. They are even setting up the steam table in that school cafeteria, bringing in whatever someone has sent in. I don't mind saying we have visions of Styrofoam trays of chicken or ribs. It keeps us going through the long afternoon.

I try to find a way to scrunch up with the book, find some halfway comfortable way to sit or lie and read. At least the time will pass. It is getting harder to make small talk with each other. We are just plain worn out, shows what shape we over forty ladies seem to be in.

My book is a bright green hardback with flowers on the front, *Ginseng and the Plants that Make You Money*. Well there would be a new skill for me at least, I chuckle to myself. I look at the pictures of the plants and flowers and think how many it would take of those to make any money. None could be found on the streets of Trenton, I'll wager. I flip it closed until the cover pops back open and I see some writing inside the cover. Feels kind of wicked to read someone else's thoughts, but I do. Whoever the writer is has nice writing with green ink, and so I read it, "When the time is right you will see a path. If you follow it, there you will find your destiny." So simple, I think, why can't everything be that simple? Destiny... that is just what I called it a few hours ago.

I looked around the room at the mass of people doing the best they can in this emergency, many of them knowing they may have nothing to go back to, may have family and friends that did not make it, beloved pets left behind. It is a heavy thought. I hand the book over to Charlene who silently reads the inscription and then hands it to Mary. We three just look at each other; then look around at all our roommates in the gym, knowing that our lives have changed in this experience. There is no point in saying it. We know each of us will have a different path now, whatever it may be. I don't know mine yet, all I've lost is a vocation, and a vacation. I knew the others well enough to know they have no clue of any path besides getting home alive. I can see it in their faces. Perhaps this experience will make for a positive difference in our lives when we get home. We may, indeed, take another path. Time will tell, there's that word again. Time.

That night they have us form a long line, lead us outside the gym door. We walk a few doors down to another entrance as the rain blows. It is cold, dark, and rainy but feels good to see the outside again. Several police guards stand on duty as we pass. It is obvious they do not want anyone to leave yet, it all feels very regimented. We are in the school cafeteria now and the ever present line moves through for sandwiches again. This time with hot meat choices, fruit, milk, chips, condiments, then back to the gym and the hard floor. They have done everything they can for normalcy in this situation. It is good to stretch the legs, even standing in line. Back in the gym someone has managed to cover the high windows that were broken. Everyone settles back in while the children play games. Other young people have gotten together playing cards or talking. Friendships have been made by this second day and by now information is filtering in.

Panama Beach was only hit with heavy damage on one end. The worst of the hurricane has hit Panama City and the surrounding towns hard with devastating damage. We hear guards and others talk about the amount of damage to the entire area. One town up the coast, Mexico Beach, was flattened. It's hard to dredge up a picture of that. I hope everyone got out. Suburban Lynn Haven took terrible damage. We heard later that twenty-six people died in the massive destruction in the Panhandle.

You could hear the chatter grow as the word spreads in the gym. Residents will not know if they have a home until they are permitted to go to find out, so they ask questions to anyone they can corral about the areas. Exhaustion and worry are on everyone's face as the reality becomes clear. While we are safe, devastation is everywhere. Those with cars can now leave the next morning if they want to, we do want to. What they don't say is that it will be hard to head out of town. The beach and many other areas are blocked off with police guards. Trees are down and block roads everywhere. We get that head-ups from the police guards outside. That's how we knew it must be pretty bad out there.

I go to the Red Cross table, ask if I can keep the ginseng book when we leave, that I might research it for a job, or open a store. The volunteer I talk to says she does not think they would miss one book; they get donations from used bookstores. I hand her two hundred dollars we three ladies have pooled together, our vacation spending money. We see the need in this area, firsthand. We ask that it be used locally by the Red Cross for more sleeping mats, cots, toys for scared, bored children. We feel gratitude for the Red Cross and the protection we have been given in a scary time. More importantly, the Red Cross will need to be here in the years to come to protect more people like us.

Then we are on our way after glancing back at our roommates who may need to stay there several more days. We feel lucky to have grabbed our bags before we left the beach. It would be days before anyone can get there again due to the massive downed trees between there and the beach.

Our hotel and area have not even been hit, we learn, but it was just a fluke of nature that it did not. We didn't count on the fact, as we drive off, that we will not be able to find gas, food or a place to stay for a hundred miles. In fact, we only get forty miles away when we have car trouble. Mary's brakes are soft, lots of stops for downed trees and rubble. No gas and not a motel room that hasn't been booked by people outrunning the storm. All rooms are gone, in use due to the hurricane.

We coast into a Walmart where the police are handing out free cases of water to the many displaced people in the area. They cannot assist with our situation until more help is sent into this rural town. We are sunk. Then the cop tells us he can take us to the shelter they have, and so that is what we do.

It is a country town. Most of the people in the shelter have been rescued from miles around after the hurricane. Many are in stages of illness and advanced age. Some on life support, some crippled. We have witnessed the massive damage to trees, homes, and land along the way. Trees look like they have been peeled leaving giant toothpicks twenty feet tall, the ones that weren't severed three feet from the ground. One crippled lady tells me she was left behind in the storm by an uncaring landlord who lives next door. She crawled to get in her bathtub to survive, holding her phone, and waited out the storm. Her rental house is gone but she survived and was rescued because she kept the phone with her. She has no place to go.

Other stories are much the same. They are not injured but need instant medical care, and a place to lay their heads. It gives one a sense of the stigma and misery of those left behind to live out life alone, even in a catastrophe. It is an eye opener for each of us to share the space with these poor and helpless souls, and their lot in life. All cots and medical supplies are needed for them. Everyone in the shelter who is able helps everyone else who is not. This is human kindness under its greatest test, and challenge.

All together we are in the two shelters a week as the whole area must rebound from the damage. They finally are able to get us gas for the car parked at Walmart, and we leave friends we have made the last few days, and our other friends in the Red Cross.

We drive a long way seeing the devastation Hurricane Michael has brought to the area. It will take a long time for life to become normal again along the Panhandle coast and inland.

In our escape from danger Charlene and I have had many discussions about our situations. She has never worked but is expecting a large settlement from her recent divorce, while I am now unemployed. She will have the capital and I have the business and computer skills. We have decided to open a florist shop, after reading about all the flowers and herbs in the ginseng book. We will have herbs for herb gardens, maybe even a little ginseng.

We three also decided to become Red Cross volunteers as we saw, firsthand, the important and vital work they do. As for the book, *Ginseng and the Plants that Make You Money*, it has gone to one of our exotic flower suppliers who says he always wanted to hunt for ginseng. He's from New Jersey and promises me the book and the message in it will go someplace where others can find it, a place where others might find their destiny, like us, in a time when they most need it.

In the meantime, I have found my new path, just as the message predicted, including a new love who also is a Red Cross volunteer. As I tell him, "all I needed to do was recognize the path to find my destiny, even in a hurricane."

Chapter Four

January, 2019
Brooklyn, New York
Kristie

I walk slowly on the ice-covered streets to my job at the Book Bin. Luckily, my boots have a good tread on bottom, this would be a sure fall with them in this weather. I'm not in a hurry to go the two blocks. I am trying to savor the fresh air and snowflakes landing on my face. How fortunate I was to have found my flat this close to work, even if it is just one room with kitchenette. It's all I need. Comfortable, clean, and one good window that looks down on the bustle of the street.

I love my job at the used bookstore, because I love books and have a constant supply of them at my disposal, and I have my own office that's quiet. It has a window on the main bookroom with its many back-to-back bookcases with titles telling the customer where to look for what genre they want.

It's my job to sort the hundreds of books brought into trade, or boxes from many estates where families have had to get rid of them after a death. It's an important job as jobs go. Nothing worse than looking for a favorite genre and finding a mish-mash of other books stuck in wrong slots. Bicycling, instead of mystery, cooking instead of history. Time is always an element of concern for lunch hours and being in a hurry to get home after work. So, there is a certain pride that comes with special steps one takes for the customer.

I have bins that are sorted for the night staff to put in the proper places, not scattered around the store. The old customers know exactly what they want and where to find it. It is a habit, as I have found, and it is appreciated by those who have a half hour for lunch, a commute home after work, etc. People want to find the new mysteries, the collectable Louis L'Amour, or Stephen King book, or the few romances they have never read. It is difficult if you have no time to browse. I am a valued employee, or so the boss tells me. There is a reason I took the job. I have mastered the art of disappearing in my little office. I am what some people would call a 'plain Jane,' as insulting as that would be to many people. It's what my mirror tells me plus the lack of male attention. I have always been the buddy, the understanding one when the guys had girl trouble. Oh, I'm not ugly, my features are just average and just seem to go together in a way that makes a nondescript, plain face. I've known it for years, gotten used to it from school years on. No one has ever said as much, but they didn't have to.

You'd be surprised to see how telling the way people look at you is. After years of what I would say are dismissive looks and averted eyes, it is easy to disappear. You simply don't look at people's faces, or look them in the eye, and then it is easy for them to ignore you.

Ten years of ballet and modern dance made me think I could come to New York and work at the many ensemble dance opportunities, but it ended up that I was too tall for ballet work, and on other auditions who do you think they wanted in the chorus line? Pretty blondes with long hair. I saw sympathy in their eyes when they told me I was an advanced dancer... but. They didn't have to say more.

So, after two years I stopped trying to fit in and started looking at the reality of my life. That was right here in this used bookstore. The job is perfect for me. No one wants to feel bad about themselves every day so why put yourself into a situation where you do? At least that's the way I look at it. I have my books, my comfortable job, even if it is not the greatest salary, and my self-respect. My greatest enjoyment is the access to travel books. The pictures and learning about places all over the world. I have first grab at all the new ones that come in, and anything else I want. Historical fiction is my other preference, and the classics so, this is the life I have chosen in my thirties. Let's just say I've adapted, and my library degree has been a skill to use here. Those techniques have kept this bookstore popular, if I do say so myself.

There really is nothing I would rather be doing except travelling, which would be too expensive to do on my salary, but I expect to do some in the coming years. Until then I have my travel books and a small savings.

I wave to the boss in his cubby behind the counter and unlock my office door. This is 'no man's land' except for him. I see several large boxes waiting for me, plus half-empty bins that the night staff has not picked up yet. They need to work a little faster and not take so many breaks. As I work, I glance out my window to the bookshelves and see who comes to the same shelves, who likes the classics, the mysteries, and the travel. They look to find the new ones I have put back after reading them. We know each other and they wave to me as they see me watching. I nod to them, a signal that there are new ones there, and get a thumb-up back. I know they will have a good night with a new book or two.

This may sound unremarkable to some, but that is how you keep a good customer coming back. Everyone appreciates personal attention, even from me with my mousy brown hair and average face that turns no heads. Some of our customers are 'plain Janes' too, faces or figures, or both. They have their own rituals and reasons for spending time at the bookstore. It's a good way to meet men. If they linger long enough someone with their interest in books may start talking to them. If I run out of work, I watch this mating dance through my window. And sometimes they come back in as a couple. Occasionally some handsome, well-dressed man comes in and stops at the travel section. I fantasize about where he may be going. He catches me looking and waves. One comes in quite often. I have chosen two or three books just for him on his usual Saturday visit, made sure the best staffer got that bin to shelve. I like watching his surprised look when he sees them. And he always takes them home with him.

It is winter. With its darkness I feel a bit depressed. It is dark in the office except for the bright gooseneck lamp on my desk, dark walking home, and dark in my little apartment. I am glad I have brought some travel books home. I don't feel like heavy reading. I usually do that on weekends. I need another lamp for this room, so I'll go shopping Sunday. Maybe get some new eye shadow or lipstick to cheer myself. But who for? I might call in sick Monday, but I never do. Go to the art museum. That sounds good, but the books would just pile up in great numbers until I sorted them. I entertain myself with books about the Tower of London, and the French Riviera.

Monday again. I have washed my hair, put on a cheerful red checked blouse to wear with jeans. The boss doesn't notice either one, but he comes in my office and wants to talk about scheduling, even though he has stacked my desk, and the floor, with boxes of books that came in. I've accumulated three weeks of vacation, he says. He can't afford me taking over a week at a time, so I need to give him set dates when I'll be taking these weeks. A few days at a time would be better for him, he says. It's only January I tell him. He knows "but the night help will have to split doing the sorting if you are not here, and you can't be gone in the summer," he tells me. "That's when the kids are in for comic books and Harry Potter stuff."

He wants me to hand in my chosen times by next week. He's having scheduling problems. I might have to pinch hit at stacking too. Walking home later I begin to have a panicky feeling. I make myself breathe slower. What would I do for two or three days at a time? It's not enough time to travel anywhere. And I may have to work in the bookroom too. That means different clothes and makeup everyday just in case. I might lose my job if I don't comply. I can feel the stinging tears as I walk in my door. I could start working part-time on the days I take off, or volunteer somewhere. I could go to the library on time off. It is too much to think about. I've got a week to figure it out but this is not setting well with me the more I consider what he is demanding.

Tuesday now, and a few more boxes came in besides the ones left from yesterday. Good, I'll be too busy to think about orders from the boss. Three weeks. You'd think he would be grateful for an employee that takes no time off when so many other people wrangle days off all the time. It would take all my savings plus what he owes me, to even go to the places I want to see. I need to get busy and sort instead of worrying. I grab a box and here are two cookbooks, one a collectable Julia Child, *Mastering the Art of French Cooking*. I lay it aside for the boss to price, as it's a very collectable item, and then a pile of the romances which I lay in their bin. Here's gardening, here's *The History of Venice* and some books on Italy. I see a green covered hardback book, must be from the gardening person. I've seen her books before. A field of lavender flowers on the front... it is *Ginseng and the Plants that Make You Money*. I look at the pictures inside. What bin would I put this in? Nature? Gardening? Occupations? I put it in the gardening bin and whoever stacks it can decide. It's on top of the other gardening book. I pick them up and the front of the green one flips open to the inside cover, first page. Another gift, another dedication. This one has pretty writing. I take a moment to read it because the green ink has interested me. 'When the time is right, you will see a path, if you follow it, there, you will find your destiny.' I read it again to let it sink in, then sit back in my chair and think about it. Is this the right time for me for anything? Is there another destiny instead of sitting in this little office, in my thirties, my last young years?

I stuff the pretty green book in the drawer because I must get this work done, but my mind never leaves the message while I sort the books. I wonder who left the message, and why? Why didn't they sign their name to it? It must have been a gift, but someone has given the book away or sold it. How could they do that with such a wonderful message? Did they take the advice? Did they find their path? I keep doing the work, but my body is tingling just thinking about the message. Could this message be for me? Stranger things have happened. Is the universe trying to tell me something? If so it's about time. But it is simply ridiculous to be carrying on about it. I need to pay attention to what I am doing.

I tackle a box of the ever-rotating romances, sort the many well-known writers that seem to churn out love stories for women who hope to meet Mr. Right, expect a new life and riches. They shouldn't be mocked for it, but they do sit at home instead of going out and finding someone real. I'm no better. In fact, I'm even more desperate, so I just read about places instead of romance.

I pull the green book out again. 'When the time is right, there will be a path...' It rolls over my tongue like honey. What a fool I've been. I've let the world beat me down... given up, but we homely girls don't have to go by the world's rules, do we? I don't have to sit in my little room until it becomes a prison. I can do better than this! I can get a loan, or sell Dad's coin collection he left me, add it to my savings, take jobs wherever I go to pay expenses on the fly. What price would be too much to pay to find your destiny? I can get a makeover — better hair and make-up, even a nose job if I want it, then get some nice clothes. I always had a good figure, or so I'm told. I can go to Greece, see the Parthenon, or France, and the Louvre. I can go anywhere, take my expensive camera, take pictures, come back and sell them. Well, I may even not come back!

I'm following this path that's right in front of me, I see it clearly the more I realize it is possible. Who knows where it might lead? This is not ridiculous! It's a choice, it's my choice. It is a long time coming, too long. It just took a message from someone who knew the answer, surely wanted others to know the answer. The answer is on the path right in front of me. I'm already walking it.

I pick up my jacket, shoulder bag, the green book, go into the store. Aisle ten... travel and tourism. I place the green book with its message of hope right smack in the middle of the eye-level row in travel and tourism. It's in the wrong shelf for the right reason! Here you are, this is for you, whoever you turn out to be, who looks at the places to go so longingly. 'Now, Voyager,' it's your turn too. Bette Davis would have been proud of both of us. She didn't take any crap in her life, and neither will I.

I head to the front counter where the boss is doing his monthly books. 'Good timing,' I think. "Hi, Roger, will you please send my three-week vacation paycheck to my address? Damon knows the job and can train others, just hire a worker to take his job, and he can step right into my job. I quit. I'm leaving now, but I'll send you a postcard when I get to Europe. Ciao! I've got a date with Destiny, and I have a feeling I'm going to like him just fine!"

Chapter Five

Indianapolis, Indiana
March 2019
Paul

While more of the Trump staff await sentencing to find out how long they will be in prison I sit here doing my own time, in real time. I'm sure, just like me, they never thought it would happen to them. Who does? I never thought I would end up number 4248126 in the Indiana State pen. I'm on hold in Indy before being transferred to Michigan City, which will be my permanent home. And speaking of life's little wrong turns, that is what I'm serving. Life — the rest of my life. I know when this happened the biggest shock was to my ego; it was like, how'd I get here? Not me, I'm one of the good guys! Well that is BS, I'm not one of the good guys, I'm one of the stupid guys. One of the 'I'm not gonna get caught, and then I'll never do it again' guys, one of the 'they'll never be able to pin it on me' guys. But they did…. Now I'm just one of the 'I screwed up my whole life' guys.

It takes a couple of years before you are ready to

admit that. Until then it's 'everyone else's fault.' You tried but no one helped you, no one else understood. Of course, as it usually goes, anyone who tried to help I took advantage of. Others were 'squares or nerds,' losers. Now, of course, I know who was 'the nerd' the 'loser.' None of this so-called soul searching helps much with all the time in the world to think about it day in and day out. I passed the reality phase a few years back, finally figured out that coping with life in prison is like a death, like the stages of death, your own or someone you love. First, there's denial, then anger, then there's the bargaining with everyone, especially the judge. Depression follows, and finally, acceptance, of your new lot in life.

The reality is the same because you bounce back and forth in all these stages. You backslide, especially in here with all the time in the world to think of how you will never get out. It's an extra punishment. In my case a lifelong one.

I'm just as angry as the first day, mostly at myself, and certainly depression is an ongoing state. I have accepted it but accepting doesn't change anything, it just lets the reality sink in a little deeper.

Oh yeah, I learned this from reading. Some of us read all the time. If I didn't, I would have to stare at the grubby walls of my six by ten home, or the exercise yard outside, or even the faces of the other men that are etched with their own horror stories.

If this is my fate, I can at least live life through others, their books of travel, family. I can build a pretend future based on their lives. It has truthfully meant more to me than my life outside ever was except for one word. Freedom. That I will never have again, so I need to find it in the books, and my mind.

I have a job here of course, laundry, but I can't wait to get back to my bunk and go to China, or Switzerland to climb a mountain, Kentucky to fish, walk the streets of London with Sherlock. I'd like to read 'The Stand' again but someone swiped it out of the library here, or better yet, any of King's new books.

If I hadn't come to acceptance, I'm sure I would have found some way to 'check out,' so maybe this is acceptance. I do think I am a different man from the one who came in here, because of the books. But that other man is gone now. Gone and left me to do his time.

Time. If you think yours is just flying by, think of what it must be like in here. For guys who will get out someday it mercilessly drags, day after day. Time simply stops, ceases to exist. If you are never going to get out, each one is the same and never going to be any different.

And so, I pass the time with my books. They are all friends who make no judgments about me and are with me as long as I open them. I can go anywhere myself, or just listen to their stories. Here is an oddity that most people would not know. Sometimes there is an extra benefit from the books that come from the outside; I smell the pages where the readers' hands have held them. A faint aroma of perfume is the very best, believe me, but a good day, that's when you can detect the smell of greasy hamburger. I get a welcome memory of my dad if someone has used Old Spice, cooked bacon. That may sound weird to some, but it can fill up a long night just fine. Time for 'lights out' now. I'm out of reading material. Preacher's gonna be here tomorrow. Hope he will bring me some good books this month. I've had to reread those I had from him this month.

Saturday

"Preacher's here." The guard yells in the cellblock. "He's in the chapel." I hear my door buzz open and grab the books I return to him every month, head to the chapel. I wonder how many inmates he visits in the jail, or the women's prison here in Indy. I never thought to ask him. There he is, just like clockwork, every month I have been here.

"Hey, Preach good to see you again!" We shake hands and have a quick prayer. I see he brought me several books this time. Of course, I am thrilled, and tell him so. He stacks them in front of me. "Thanks a million, I was starting over on these." I hand him the three from this last month.

"Don't you go to the prison library, Paul?"

"Aw, read about all of them," I say. "All the interesting ones, I may have to start on the cooking ones someday!" I laugh and so does he. He's got his Saturday clothes on today instead of a suit. Jeans and a tee shirt. Saturday is his day to come from Bloomington and waste his valuable time with a jailbird like me, and whatever other parishioners he visits. "If I don't say it enough, Preach, I am so grateful to get the books, and see you every month."

He claps a meaty hand on my shoulder, towering over me in a heavy muscled six-foot frame. "I wouldn't be here if I did not think you have value and purpose. You're a smart man Paul, and there's a lot of goodness in you." I feel my eyes getting a tad misty and pull over the stack of books.

"How's the writing going Paul?" he asks.

"Well, here's what I was writing last night, thought you might like to read it." He busies himself with it while I look at the books he's brought.

"Oh, great, a Stephen King book! Thanks, Preach.

He nods as he reads. I continue looking. I see a book on psychology, one on ancient Egypt and, a green hardback, "*Ginseng, and the Plants that Make You Money.*"

"Well, it sounds interesting," I say, "lots of pictures,

too. All the fun of nature without the ticks and mosquitoes." I wisecrack.

He smiles but keeps reading while I look at the pictures. Finally, he says, "Paul, this is quite good, really good. I'd like to see more."

I tell him, "Thanks," but I think he's just being nice about it. "I told you I was getting desperate for something to read, I had to resort to writing myself something to read. I have visions of you getting sick and missing our visit some month, then no books."

"Oh no, I'd get some to you some way, have a little faith, Paul, the Lord'll provide." He grins. "Why don't you see if you can get more books, and newer ones, for the prison library, like that Morgan Freeman movie?"

"That's just Hollywood, Preach. Remember there was a crooked warden in that one, our guy is straight as an arrow here... but I loved that movie, didn't you?"

He nods, "I sure did, but I'm getting the books I bring from a used bookstore. I bet a few of them would donate books if anybody would ask. I didn't think of it myself until now, they are constantly turning over new books too. I just take these back and get other ones, but back to the writing, I'm serious, you have a real knack for it. If you want to continue, maybe even use this effort for a book, I'll see you get a ream of paper, maybe some pens and pencils too. If you come up with something as good as this, I will take it to a friend of mine, a Lit teacher at

IU. He may be able to recommend it to someone."

Well, I am stunned. "Are you serious, you'd do that?"

He puts his hand on the well-worn Bible he carries, "My word on it if it's as good as this."

I shake my head at his offer. "Well, I sure have the time to try, don't I?"

His face is serious now. "You know, I hate to make this a cliché, but if you applied yourself to this you could actually make some money, maybe even help some other people who might make the same mistakes, and think about this. Laws may change, or authorities may be influenced. A published book would sure look good on your record, along with good behavior, people to speak for you. And what about a different prison job, based on your skills, something to do with books or time to write? I see so many possibilities...."

I am speechless, now. None of this sounds possible but it's great to think about it. "I'll think about it," I say, "Thanks for the pep talk, you should be a preacher!" I tease.

"Well, there's no guarantee about any of it, but what an accomplishment even if you just do it for yourself, for it to be on your record here and the job possibility. You know how I came to be a minister?" he asks. "What inspired me, besides my faith I mean."

I shake my head.

"Interestingly enough, it was a writer. He was from

here, from Indy in fact. I didn't know him, read some of his work in the science community some years back. He founded a group called the United States Psychotronic Association, evidently for scientists to work together in the different fields of energy that were not mainstream at the time. You know I'm sort of in the 'unknown energy' field myself. Anyway, his name was J.G. Gallimore. I looked him up after I saw a quote of his on the Mir Space station website several years back. The quote is, 'Image creates desire, you will what you imagine.' In other words, Paul, you make happen what you see in your mind, you make what you desire come to being. The image has a follow through to happen. You have willed it to exist. I was not a public speaker; it was difficult to find the confidence to do it, to pass on in sermons what I believe. The quote stuck in my mind as a pretty inspiring idea. I wanted to convey my own thoughts on the scriptures so much that I could begin seeing myself do it, and it became easier. It seems we do create our own lives with every thought or action we take, good or bad. It took me awhile to apply this new information to my life, but it was a breakthrough moment and many people saw the difference — because it made all the difference. That's pretty heavy to think about, isn't it?"

I sigh, "More so than you can imagine, Preach."

"So, keep this in mind as you think about it, what is

writing except imagination in words you will to be on the paper?"

"I guess you are right, Preach, yeah, that is absolutely right."

He stands up and grabs me in a bear hug, "Paul, somehow I think you have much to say to this world when you are ready to say it, I will help you in any way I can."

I shake his big hand "You've been a good friend," I tell him and mean it. "I won't forget it when I leave here."

The buzzer sounds and our hour meeting is over for another month. He picks up the three books from this last month, motions to the guard to buzz him out, waves over his shoulder and is gone. I grab my five book stack and head back to my cell with much to think about. My step is a little lighter because I leave the meeting with a little ray of hope when I have none.

That night I start on the Stephen King book. It's an old one. *Insomnia*, about a man who cannot sleep. Lord knows I've been there in these last few years. I wonder where King will go with this, but I throw it aside and lay there thinking I might write some sentences on how I got here, but it's too depressing to start just now. I can't think who even would be interested in that. There are thousands of stories in here more telling than mine, much more horrible, much more inspirational too.

I don't want to go back to my lean, mean, even obscene years. People want happy stories, not criminal stories, don't they? I begin to doubt myself after these years of self-examination. I begin to doubt Preach, too, who means so well, but he is doing the job he has given himself unselfishly. He's been a friend, an inspiration to better people than me, a confidante; most important to him, he's fulfilled his work to one of the sinners. He's good at his job. I lapse into my negative thinking and do nothing but read the King book. It's a good way to lose the world in your mind and I have become very good at it.

Preach was as good as his word. In a very few days I have gotten a package from him. It's rather like Christmas, although I know, by the weight of it, what it contains. So, this is what a ream of paper looks like. It's a precious bundle. Scary, but precious all the same. There's a pack of pencils and even a little plastic pencil sharpener. He must have pulled strings to get that contraband through the scanners.

There is a short note from the preacher saying he has written a letter to the warden about me, requesting he be able to send materials to me from time to time. He has also written down the Gallimore quote in case I forget it. The idea of it had been on my mind but not the exact words. "Image creates desire, you will what you imagine." I take the tape off an old newspaper clipping someone had sent me with a picture of a former girlfriend getting married. I stick the quote over it. I need to ask for tape as I have the paper now. I could draw a picture or two for the wall or locker. It'd be something to look at anyway. I lie down and stare at the quote. The paper with the writing on it is an image. It does nothing unless I do something with the image, the words put in my mind. I must be the one to will it to do what I want, but what do I want? I want to be out of here. I want to start all over again. I want to have control over my life, not live every day by a buzzer. But it seems impossible. It is a fixed situation in time, one that I willed myself or it wouldn't be.

I have trapped my own foot in a snare. That's what I get from this quote. I willed what I imagined, only it was the wrong image and I got caught. How would I think I could get out of this trap? The words of Preach feel good. They're pretty, they're hopeful words. They made me feel anything is possible but here I sit in my reality. It's a negative one. I see it in every face, in every slumped shoulder, every harsh word said to every person from every other person.

I jump up and put the ream of paper on the top shelf of the locker and close the door. I want to block out all feeling and read. I look through the books again and grab the green hardback, *Ginseng and the Plants that Make You Money*. I throw it on my bunk and get a stale cookie kept from some past meal. I sit and study each picture of open fields of flowers, read that this one is lavender, the one on the front of the book. Thousands of purple spiky flowers in this field. I read the text on how lavender is used in so many ways. I try to smell the page but nothing there, just the smell of hopefulness, maybe, from the people that had it before me, those trying to make money the honest way. I flip back and forth looking at the strange plants that just look like weeds to me. I'll have to read it later to see what those weeds are. This really is a great book. All those fields have roads that take you somewhere. I know I will spend many hours reading about what each herb and flower will do for humans one way or another. Suddenly the front has flipped to the front page and I see writing in a beautiful hand, that has to be a woman's writing. I smell it and there is a wonderful fragrance. Even the green ink is a potent smell. Someone's hands have had a perfume or some other fresh scent on them. I could smell this forever and never get tired of it. I read the words written there. 'When the time is right you will see a path, if you follow it, there you will find your destiny.' Oh, what a shock to read this, these few words so important, so needed. Tears roll down my face. I wonder if Preach has seen this. If not, I must tell him in a letter. I must tell him this message is for me, that in spite of everything, even my negative thoughts, I know this is the right time, this is the right path.

I know I will take it, accept whatever destiny holds for me, in here or out there. I start sharpening several pencils, with this action I have a new image in my mind as I smell the wood I have shaved off the pencil. It is of that field of lavender, it's as real to me as this pencil in my hand. I can almost smell the real flowers shown in the book. Suddenly I am excited about my new destiny, wherever it leads. This field of lavender is the mental path I take now. It's my first step for a new kind of freedom. Somehow, I know I will never look back.

Chapter Six

Bloomington, Indiana
June 2019
Heavenly

I didn't know college was going to be so hard, and I didn't know a freshman would have their hands full with eighteen hours and a part time job. Here I am stuck with an overload at Indiana University, a part time job, another high school class to finish because I never took Government, a high school requirement for undergrads, and a commitment for one hour per week of extra credit in the community instead of a traffic citation. And when do I study? Whenever I get a precious hour to myself. It's not working. Sociology, Psychology, History, Science, early childhood education, and French. Holy Maird! And the book expenses are just unbelievable.

I don't know what I was thinking. I should have listened to the counselor, but I thought that this would be the breeze that high school was. Guess I thought the world would be my oyster once I got started, that I could graduate in three years with a liberal education and then decide what I want to do. Looks like I got the empty shell instead of the oyster. The way I'm going I will flunk out of freshman year, and then what? The extra credit with the nursing home every Saturday is a relief compared with my hectic schedule, and then I go to work at the Union building on campus.

I enjoy the time I spend with Mr. Hicks at the nursing home, but he is rather a downer lately. I can tell he's in lots of pain even though he says nothing. I think I cheer him up though, bring him books every week, sometimes other things. On Christmas I gave him and the poor old man next to him socks, what I could afford.

He reads books like most people read magazines, so I keep up by checking out library books when I grab the time to study. He sure knows his history, watches it all on TV too. My visits with him fly; strangely enough they have become golden moments.

I'm nineteen years old and what I look forward to is time with a seventy-year-old man. I've earned my credit, already, but I would miss him if I stopped coming. I tell him about my college troubles; so far, he just listens and gives no advice. But advice is what I need, and time is running out. I need solutions now. I need to tell someone I am in way over my head and the semester is finished, so I will go all summer. Desperation is staring me in the face; I have nowhere to turn, and no one to care. Like Mr. Hicks, I feel hopeless. We are quite a pair.

Bloomington, Indiana
June 2019
Jason

June, wonderful Indiana June, is calling from my picture window here in the room. It really is 'busting out all over' and making me wish for younger days, much younger, when I climbed the elm trees just like the one that keeps me company here every day. Even the tree feels better this spring with its waving limbs, and full-bodied leaves. It should make me feel better as in past years, but it doesn't.

I feel a mean depression sinking in, but it will take care of itself before long. Today I cannot afford to indulge in it. I shake it off as I have so often because I need my wits about me today. I look over at my comatose roommate so peaceful, as always, and I envy that peace. He's got no pain, no worries, no memories to push him into a regret that has no remedy. He cares nothing for a family that no longer comes to see him, or the gargantuan cost of his bed and care. He's where what my plans will lead to if all goes right.

The Doc is here right on time for his morning rounds. He looks at old Frank lying there, checks his eyes and vitals, writes on the white 'chalkboard' they have now. No more clipboards at the end of beds. They leave notes and instructions for the next guy or gal — actually it's for the nurses on each shift. The black marker words at least entertain me for a minute or two as I try to interpret the directions he leaves. He is already glued to the window as he comes to me, drawn to the warm spring weather luring him to eighteen holes, when he can make time on his busy schedule.

He is all business as usual and I hope he does not notice my grimace of pain as he checks me over. "What's your pain level today, one to ten," he asks, and those are the words I want to hear.

"Pretty bad, I've been asking for a higher dose. This is a 'Niner' day."

"It would help if you went to therapy more than once a week," he tells me.

"Yeah, I know, that therapy can't help a hip that has degenerated as long as mine, and the pain doing the therapy is unbearable."

He watches the men mowing grass out the window.

"I know it's bad, we'll contact the VA again to see if they'll pay for a replacement hip, and a new artificial leg that will help you begin to be mobile again. Things have changed there again. Meanwhile, I'll up the meds some but we can't have you being a zombie with it. You know you're addicted after so many years of pain, and surgeries. That's just a huge problem everywhere. It's one of things that Trump is gaga about, trying to keep his base pimped up. It has made it hard for all medical facilities and pharmacies. We have firm directions from Washington's programs to cut dosages because of the ongoing problems of overdoses, and street sales. But there will be some for you and other chronic sufferers, like you. The therapy will help you adjust. I'll tell them you will come, and to take it easy with you."

I take a deep breath as he leaves and glance over at old Frank. I have succeeded with the Doc. He would be surprised to know just how long I have gone without meds; it was true about the pain level. The therapy is excruciating but I could stand the ordeal if I had to, but it won't take long now with the extra dosage he is giving me. I can stand the pain a little while longer until I have enough to check out of this bed, this misery. Unless I go to therapy, that is.

No one has discovered my stash under the mattress, but I need to move them to the aspirin bottle on my table in case they decide to turn the mattress. I'm leaving nothing behind after living in this chair so many years, nothing but a little lady who comes to cheer me every week when she should be having fun with people her own age.

Heavenly, that's her name, and she is. My family disowned me long ago when I, regretfully, left them all behind. I really don't feel sorry for myself. It's long past. The truth is, so many of us had PTSD before it was diagnosed that we wrecked many lives, including our own. I have felt I am just taking up space on this Earth for many useless years. What is the point of living in pain? I am obsolete, realistically, and if I live another ten years nothing will be any different. I will still be in this rolling trap after a few more surgeries. I have never recovered from the loss of the leg, mangled hip, pelvic injuries compliments of damage in Viet Nam, booze, and weed from two deployments. Forty some years later that is the truth, that and being in long term hospital care. I had a life as a young man but that all went away, all except for a series of wheelchairs which have evolved more than I have in forty years. I'm set to do this thing when I have enough pills to make sure I do the job right. I don't plan on joining Frank over there.

Doing the job right reminds me of my Grandpa Charlie all those years ago. He was a character, rough around the edges, a Navy man through and through. I can hear him now. In the morning he'd yell, "Wake up and piss, boy, the world's on fire." If I didn't follow his orders, I'd hear 'All jobs big or small-do them well or not at all,' and he drilled me all the time, 'Once a job you have begun, never quit until it's done.' These old adages must be some old Navy recruit training.

He was rough but he was fun. I think I got my love of history from him talking about war days from 'the big one.'

My other grandfather was ex-Navy too. He was quieter, more of a thinker, except when he liked a little too much of the 'hair of the dog.' Then, he clapped and laughed when he got me to stand up at the age of three or four and sing 'Queenie the queen of the Burlesque Show.' Oh, how he got a kick out of that.

One day when I was about twelve, he told me, "You know, Jason, we'd be awful stupid to think we are the only ones in the universe, all by ourselves, don't you think?" I thought he was trying to talk to me about God. I remember I just nodded, was embarrassed, and didn't answer. Years later I wondered if he might be talking about people from other planets instead, UFO's, that would have been cool. I still wonder all these years later. H. Kenneth was Granddad's name. I never heard anyone call him anything but H. Kenneth, and I never knew his first name. I guess I never will know unless I run into him in the great beyond. That's not going to be too far away. I'll miss the history on this little television in my room though, I should say 'our room,' but Frank wouldn't know one way or another. I'll miss the Oak Island treasure hunters in the next seasons, truth be known, miss getting to see what they find each time or the real treasure, whatever 'Bobby dazzlers' show up. That history they uncover will be a shock to the world, history recovered, and religion uncovered.

I will miss the only other bright spot in this dulled

life of pain. She comes here, once a week, like clockwork. Heavenly, that's her name. Brings me cookies and history books, the only bright spot.

Heavenly, the college student just starting in life. What a name, huh? Well, she does look like an angel and has been one to this old man all these last months. I envy her, so young, so much ahead of her. She brings a few golden moments to me when I can forget the pain. I do forget about it. I wouldn't show my pain to her for anything. For that hour I am not constantly thinking of the past, thinking of what I must do. Soon I will add to my saved pills, have just enough to either see what's there in the great beyond, or to join Frank over here in la-la land. Heavenly likes to talk to him when she comes. She is convinced that he can hear everything around him. Wouldn't that be something, if true? I can't say I would like that idea at all, personally, hearing but helpless. Not for me, that's why I plan on doing it right.

Speaking of the kid, there she is, right on time with an armload of books and her big smile. "Hey, Sunshine!" I greet her, and push the pain down once more, "How's dorm life? You getting to enjoy this pretty weather?"

She grins, shrugs, and drops the books on the bottom of the bed, "I'm too busy to enjoy anything, especially outside," she says, goes over to poor old Frank. "How are you today, Mr. Adams? Have they been treating you well?" She pats his arm above the covers and comes back to sit down by me. "How long have you been in the wheelchair today?" she wants to know. I tell her from breakfast till now. She nods "Let's go outside, I'll roll you out under that tree. Nobody's there."

That perks me up some. "Sure, great. I would like to feel that sun on my back. These people are too busy, so I don't ask."

She jumps up and out the door; we roll down the elevator to the exit. This is a real treat after the cold winter, nothing to look at but snow and ice. We sit under the tree, sun shining on my back. Even in the chair it feels heavenly. I laugh and tell her the little joke. She sits on the ground and picks daisies and hands me some to feel. She makes a chain of her flowers. I hold mine to my nose and smell the wildness, the life.

"You didn't answer how you were doing."

"Oh, it's not going well, I have to go all summer for make-up work or I'll flunk out for the semester, and it's more money to do it. I never have enough time to study."

"And yet you come here? Surely you have your extra credit by now, use this time to study." I see her eyes start to water.

"If I didn't come here, I don't know what I'd do, it's the only time I feel free, the only time I can get away from all these classes and problems."

"Sounds like you are having a rough time of it. How's your history class?"

She throws down her flowers. "Boring, boring, boring, I don't know how you can stand those books I bring. I just took it because my counselor told me I needed to. I brought a couple science ones this time."

"Maybe it's your teacher that's boring. Here's something I found out about history: People don't know that history is not what happened, it's what we think happened, what we've been told by the informants, bad information and urban legend, which proves to be very different than the facts that have faded in time. I'll give you an example. In grade school they teach a history that is the same year after year. What were the names of Columbus' ships? I ask her.

She answers, "The Nina, Pinta, and Santa Maria."

I shake my head, "That is incorrect," I tell her, "but that is the going history in the books. Actually, the Spanish named every ship after a saint. There really was a Santa Maria, but another one of the three was the St. Clare. The third is not known. Lost to history? Possibly the Nina and Pinta may have been names of sailor's girl friends or wives, or so the Spanish say."

She looks at me in amazement, "Really? That's very interesting. How do you know this?"

"I know because there are writers that care enough about truth in history to investigate and write about it. I like to find these books for that reason."

"One book is very famous, *A Peoples History of The*

United States. The writer is Howard Zinn and he has sold well over a million copies of that book. In it he tells the masses the real truths behind what we have been told. It was to be for the people of this country instead of the versions told by politicians and the wealthy. Did you know at one time only the wealthy in the United States could hold a political office, even vote? And did you know that Columbus was anything but a hero?"

"The same is true of so many historical facts. Archeologists have found no evidence that the Exodus ever happened, that forty thousand people were ever in the Sinai Peninsula in ancient time, as there is no trace of bones, animal or human, waste matter, pottery, or any other evidence they were ever there."

Her eyes were bigger now, "Amazing, that's all really interesting!"

"It is," I say, "and it is the tip of the iceberg of true history."

She gets to her knees to pick some wild violets under the tree, hands the little bundle of them to me. "That's not boring at all, I want to know more. You don't know it but I have a term paper I did not get done, have to make it up some way. I just kept putting it off, probably will flunk history too because of it. You know, I could do it on that book, and the other facts it uses! I thought I was finished, but I could drop other classes that are not electives. I could major in history, maybe teach a different form of it someday! It is so fascinating the way you tell it that I want other people to know about it!

"Yes, you could do all that, but you may find you have to buck the establishment, people won't accept the truth, even gracefully, I'm sorry to say. You would have to take on some severe criticism and obstacles. I am very glad I could help, but I urge caution if you are interested in doing that. I didn't know you were in so much difficulty, and very sorry to hear it."

"Well, maybe it's not as hopeless as I think. I have a long way to go before I solve my problems. I'll need to go slow. I know one thing; I'm going to find that book as soon as I leave here. You should be a history teacher yourself; if nothing else you could write your own book about it. People need to know these things!"

I laugh at her enthusiasm, it felt good to hear it and good to laugh, but little did Heavenly know this will be the last time we will talk. Her youthful enthusiasm is very refreshing, in spite of me being down all the time. "Don't forget, Zinn is not the only writer who was determined that people know the truth, the real history, there are many writers to explore, and I hope you do."

Our time is up. I can feel her reluctance to go but she jumps up. She seems to have joy with having a plan, hope for the future. Right then I decided I will leave what money I still have to this bright and giving girl with the angelic name.

We say goodbye, and I tell her if I am not in my room when she comes next week, the nurses know to give the books back to her. Heavenly's last words to me were "I'll get us some more of those writer's books for next week!" and she was gone.

The nurse came in, checked on Frank, helped me into bed. She handed me the books Heavenly had brought so I could read before dinner. One science book is on climatology which I had been very interested in, all the time in the world to watch Discovery, and Smithsonian, but I was hurting too much to read it. I throw it aside and see one with a green cover. It grabs my interest because of the field of lavender on front. Who knew lavender is so spiky, looks like a field of purple corn. I open it and buzz my bed down to lie flat, but the pain is too bad, so I grab the silver handle on the bed and turn myself away from the bad hip. This one is entitled, *Ginseng and the Plants that Make You Money.* I had to smile thinking that lots more money was being made with weeds stronger than ginseng.

The book flips over to the front page. Some pretty writing I see there, green ink from a pen with a nib, so I read it. 'When the time is right, you will see a path, if you follow it, there you will find your destiny.' Huh, it gives me chills to read something that just screams for my plan to work, my path is clear, or is it? The path I have chosen leads to oblivion, not destiny, but it's a beautiful sentiment all the same. The time seems to be right for me to go, yet is this message trying to tell me something? Do I believe in fate or alternate destiny, guardian angels? If those exist, they would stop me from checking out. Is Heavenly my guardian angel coming at this time, with her sunshine and books? The name sure fits. I was so sure I could do it, I still am still sure, but is it the right path? Or is this telling me that Heavenly is the path? A girl on her own having trouble. I helped her today, but I could do more since she has no one, it seems. And I have no one either.

I have some money and Heavenly needs money or she would not be working hard enough to be unable to study. This is not believable, though, a random message appears when I have it all figured out. She's right about one thing, I could write a book, all I need is a computer for more research, and then start writing. I'm only seventy, with a lifetime of learning in me. If she is that bored, what the hell are they teaching these kids? Does she just need a dose of the excitement she felt today? I don't know what to do with this. I read the message again and marvel at the timing of it, a coincidence? If I don't go through with it now, it doesn't mean I can't some other time.

I'll have to think about it, just not so sure now. I reach under me, get my pills under the mattress. I take one because I hurt so badly, have to admit defeat from the pain, at least today. I can't reason this out, decide to put the others in the side table drawer. It's hard to think, feel worn down, just wanting it to end. I haven't been to therapy, Doc's right on that, but I could try again. The girl seems to need me, and as much as I hate to admit it, I need her too. I shove the green book under my pillow and turn off my light. 'There you will find your destiny,' I mull over the words again and painfully turn over in the bed. Maybe I'll just sleep on this. I can decide tomorrow, anyway. Maybe I have miles to go before I sleep.

Chapter Seven

Chris
August 2019
San Francisco, California

I can't forget...the magic lady...and don't want to. The lady with the misbehaving blonde curl, with the lavender oil temples, the flowing gypsy skirt on a hot day.

Yes, she was pure magic with her quick wit and sparkly green eyes. Even the fragrances were mesmerizing in that heat. But she thinks I jilted her, no doubt, and now she seems to be gone. No name, no number. It's like losing a pet, you must to start searching immediately if you want to find them before something happens. She would not appreciate the analogy, I am sure, but the premise is correct. No telling what might happen, and I am just stuck for a few more days. One thing I can do is call that mall first thing tomorrow.

Dad's funeral had drained both of us, but it was good to see so many of their friends I had grown up around, and now their children and grandchildren. They were interested in my life, of course, especially those with the pretty granddaughters they introduced me to.

The months pass with me invited, attending a number of these 'first date' dinners of encouragement but I am not in the market. My thoughts are of one pretty woman with lavender oil on her temples. Still it is good for my mom to get out too. Meantime, I call her store number, but it is still disconnected. This is not good.

I will track her down when I go back to St. Louis, retrieve my car, close the apartment, getting away to do it right now is another matter. Who knew there were so many loose ends to tie up in a death? I make a mental note to never leave someone to do this for me in a time of stress and worry. Mom is eighty years old, full of occasional confusion and forgetfulness, adding to her grief. She would have been lost, very upset, and helpless had I not been able to be here.

In the months that have passed the people in and out have been good for Mom... She is even having a card game night with ones from her old life. Church has been important too. I hope it all continues as she is easing into her old friendships that have much more in common with her than I. Some are widows too and share their other friends with her. It's all good. Now she has a new life and must adjust. I have enjoyed the time with her, have done some investment business in the city, but it is time for me to fly the nest, once more.

It's two more weeks before I can get back to St. Louis. I, more or less, prepare Mom for my leaving for a few days. She says she is fine, and I finally tell her about the magic lady. She says I have been a fool, should have gone months ago, and so I do, with a clear mind and heart. My first stop from the plane is the mall. It's crowded with people who want to get out of August heat. August, that's right! It was a year ago that I met her. A year since Dad had died. How is this possible? I realize I have switched off my life for the past year. I wonder if it will be too late. She could even be married by now. I walk the mall looking for Perfumes and Potions, asking salesclerks as I go. No one seems to know. One lady tells me to go to the mall office, but I continue looking. I get to the opposite end with no such store. The last thing is the movie theatre. I see a sign listing the stores and hers is nowhere to be seen, but the mall office is not far. I must have passed it.

I feel failure coming on and am not willing to accept that I will not see her again. The secretary greets me, pleasantly. She says the obvious, that store is no longer in the mall. She has no more information, but I can wait and talk to the manager. She will return at two o' clock. Yes, of course I will return; in the meantime the food court beckons to me with its many aromas and I realize I have not eaten today. I kill an hour with a burger and fries, and then shop for an upscale scarf for Mom so she knows I'm thinking of her on this first trip away, but I am really thinking of a bright gypsy skirt and green eyes the color of a cat's eye marble.

I select a green and blue silk scarf, have it gift wrapped. The clerk flirts with me, asks if the scarf is for my wife. No, it's for my mom I tell her; she tells me I have a lucky mom. Time to head back to the manager. She is in the outer office, waiting for me, usher me into her office. I immediately ask about the perfume store that was here.

"Sir, Miss Marshall's contract was up with the mall. She opted not to continue it."

Ah, I think, 'Miss Marshall,' finally a name! I feel relief. "Do you know where she went?"

"No, I'm afraid that information is not for the public, I'm very sorry I can't help you."

Now I am beyond frustrated and beginning to feel panicky. "Look, Ma'am, we met a year ago, we keep missing each other. My father died and I had to leave, I must track her down."

She smiles. "I saw that movie too, wish I could help but rules are rules, you understand?"

"This is not a movie, this is two lives and one rule, do I need to bribe you?"

She gets up, opens her door, calls the receptionist into the office. "Linda, you did not hear me give this gentleman any information, did you?" Linda shakes her head. "Then you heard me when I told you the other day that this lady recently sold her store stock and decided to go to France?"

Linda shakes her head, yes, slowly looks at me and grins.

I nod, "Ma'am, I am as silent as the grave, is there anything else at all you can tell me, I am really desperate now that I hear she is no longer in the country." I wait, Linda waits, and the manager, sport that she is, reaches into a drawer and pulls out a file folder. She looks, Linda looks, I look.

"Linda, this client said two weeks ago that if I needed to contact her on any matter that she would be staying at the Hotel Maison Montgrand, for a few days. She forgot to give me the city and I don't have a phone number. Will you update this file if she calls?"

Linda nods, still grinning. The manger shakes her head, says to me, "Looks like you just missed her again, I'm so sorry."

I bounce from the chair "Don't be!" I say, "You're wonderful!" I kiss the manager, I kiss Linda, and fly out of the office.

Back at my apartment and I Google the hotel, so simple, it's in Marseille, she's in Marseille! I call the hotel and I am holding my breath.

"Bonsoir, Hotel Maison Montgrand," the male voice

answers.

"Anglais!" I say.

"No Francais!"

"Oui, Miss Marshall?" I stammer.

He says, "Oui? Eh Momento?"

He clicks off, and a lady comes on. "Oui? Miss Marshall? No, Mademoiselle is not here."

I realize I am talking loud now to long distance, "Has she checked out?"

"Monsieur, she is not here in her room. She will check out tomorrow she has said. You have called very late."

"Thank you! Thank you! I need to leave a message for her, a very important message!"

"Oui, Monsieur, please continue."

"Tell her it is Chris, from the St. Louis market! I could not get there! But I'm coming, now! Don't check out! Miss Marshall, I'm coming to the rescue!"

"Sir, please slow down."

"No, Read it back to me," I demand.

She continues.

"That's right," I say. "She must get this message as soon as possible, got any flowers there? Oui? Give them to her! I'll pay you when I get there! What? I don't care, any kind! Yes, thank you! Wait! What is her first name?" But she had hung up! Damn! I call the airport and get the soonest flight out that will take me to Marseille. It transfers in Paris in the north to go to the southern coast, then Marseille. I'll take that flight, but I will head to the airport and hope for an earlier cancellation.

Before I head out, I must call Mom. She answers and I hear several people chatting in the background, ah, that's a good thing when I have to tell my eighty-year-old mother I'm going away for God knows how long. "Mom, hi, I have found her, the woman I told you about! Yes! She's in France, Marseille. Yes, I know I was a fool to wait, Mom I must go, I hope you understand. No, I don't know when I'll be back. Yes, I know Dad would want me to. I bought you a silk scarf today, yeah, it's pretty--blue and green. I'll send it from France. French perfume? Sure Mom, this is the lady that can pick it out for you, she might even make it for you herself. Gotta go Mom and catch a flight. Yes, I know you want to see any grandkids. Yes, I promise you will. Gotta go now, I will, love you, Mom!" and I hit the off button.

Mom's going to be just fine. I make another call to arrange for someone to put my car in storage, pack up my clothes and wait for an address to ship them to me. I pack my tux and a few of my nicer sweaters and shirts, grab my passport, other important papers, head out the door for whatever life brings me, going to see my girl. And so, I go with a clear mind and heart. I'm on my way.

Marseille, France

Hotel Montgrand. It's lovely, of course, I would expect nothing less on this path I have taken. I am anxious, eager to experience the sheer excitement of this important moment. I wonder if she will even remember me. The man at the counter greets me, "Bonjour, Monsieur."

I ask for Miss Marshall's room number. He looks and comes back with the last words I want to hear. "I'm sorry, Monsieur, Mademoiselle has checked out."

"What?" I almost yell, "When?"

"It appears she checked out yesterday," the heavy accent says. "There is a message for a 'Chris,', if that is you?"

"Yes! Here is my passport." He hands me the official hotel notepaper.

"What a surprise to hear from you, Chris," it begins. "I must check out, but I will come back tomorrow to have dinner in the restaurant. I will stay until eight P.M. Thank you for the flowers. I hope we do not miss each other again." There was no signature.

I shake my head and exhale with relief. That is today, she will be back today! It is late afternoon. I book a room to grab a shower and change. This is the moment. This is the path I have taken. Will she return? Will either of us feel what we did when we met? I've come thousands of miles to answer that very question.

The restaurant is blessedly quiet with very few diners. I look around but do not see her. Then I hear a soft voice behind me and turn.

"Bonsoir, Chris," she says with a gorgeous smile. "Here you are at last, I must say it's a long time to wait for a dinner date."

I take her hand. "I have much to tell you, but first, I have waited this long year too, to find out your name. You said it was in the ginseng book, but I looked everywhere, until I lost it in a cab."

We sit down at our table and she says, "In a cab? Oh my, Chris, didn't you read the little message I always write in the front of all my books? 'When the time is right, you will see a path, if you follow it, there will be your Destiny."

"Yes, my mysterious lady, and it led me to a path I have followed all the way to France, it led me to you."

"Yes, it did..." she said, smiling her magic smile, "...and you chose the right path. Chris, my name is Destiny."

End

To the reader

Thank you for selecting my novella and traveling with a book into the lives of six people. I certainly hope you enjoyed it. If so, please encourage me with your review on Amazon. While you are there, stop by my author page and check out my other books, a novel and sequel to it, and a mystery/horror collection.

If you have not achieved your true destiny, I hope this novella will inspire you to keep watching for your path. When the time is right, you will find it.

Crossroads to Destiny
Chronicles of Jongleur, the Storyteller
The Devil on God's Mountain
Midwest Quadrille-Four Dances with Terror